# NOT IN THE MOOD

Joseph Namara Hollis

TATE

Hedgehog was sitting and thinking.
He was thinking **SO** hard
that it hurt his head.

Something just didn't feel right ...

Suddenly his doorbell rang!

Hedgehog opened the door. All of his friends were stood outside.

"Do you want to come outside and play, Hedgehog?" asked Cat.

Hedgehog thought some more.
"No, thank you," he said.

"I'm not in the mood."

"Not in the mood to play?" asked Frog.

"No." said Hedgehog. "Goodbye."
And he shut the door and sat back in his chair.

"It's better people don't see me today, not in this mood," thought Hedgehog.

DING DONG!

The doorbell rang again!

"Want to practice some cool dance moves?" asked Giraffe.

"Yeah!" said Dog. "Let's **BOOGIE!**"

Hedgehog stood aside as his friends danced through his door.

It was quite clear to Hedgehog that he was not in the mood for dancing.

The music was **VERY** loud!
"I'm not in the mood!"
shouted Hedgehog.

"Musical chairs then?"
asked Elephant.

"Remarkably similar to dancing," said Hedgehog, scratching his head.

"Let's play dress-up then?"
suggested Cat.

"Pirates!" yelled Dog.
"Astronauts?" asked Frog.

"Ninjas, spies, explorers?"
His friends went on ...

And on, and on . . .
Hedgehog wondered if he would ever be understood.

He didn't feel like being a ninja, a spy or an explorer.

Most strange of all, he didn't feel like being Hedgehog either.

"I'm really not in the mood,"
he mumbled.

He began to wonder if he would
ever feel like Hedgehog ever again.

So his friends tried to cheer him up.

"Noodles for dinner?
We can share a big, brown egg!"

Hedgehog did love his food ...

"Fishing at
Stingray Creek?"

Hedgehog did
love fishing ...

"What about your
favourite ostrich ride?"

Hedgehog did
love ostrich rides ...

But he felt
tired of it all.

Hedgehog's friends could see that they would need to try harder.

"Well, you've always wanted to go sky diving?"

"I'M NOT IN THE MOOOOD!"

Hedgehog cried, as he
soared through the sky.

He stamped his feet.

He clenched his fists.

And he bared his teeth.

"I'M NOT IN

the M.O.O.D."

Cat, Frog, Elephant, Giraffe and Dog all stared at Hedgehog. "But why not?"

Hedgehog frowned.
He looked quite
puzzled and then
he looked
very sad indeed.

"I don't know,"
he said very quietly.

"But I'm not in the
mood for anything."

“Sometimes I feel like that too,” said Frog.

“Really?” thought Hedgehog.

“Me too!” said Dog.

"It's OK Hedgehog.
We all feel that
way sometimes!"

"Let's be
*not in the mood*,
together!"

Together they sat and they talked,
and talked, and talked some more.

Sharing his feelings made
Hedgehog feel lighter.

“What will tomorrow bring?”
they wondered. Hedgehog smiled,
“No matter what happens, we’ll
always have each other.”

JH - For Little O
and all the people who
brighten our mood.

First published 2024 by order of the Tate Trustees
by Tate Publishing, a division of Tate Enterprises Ltd,
Millbank, London SW1P 4RG

www.tate.org.uk



Designer: Roanne Marner
Editor: Emilia Will
Production: Juliette Dupire



A catalogue record for this book is available from the British Library

ISBN hardback 978 1 84976 886 3
ISBN paperback 978 1 84976 909 9

Distributed in the United States and Canada by ABRAMS, New York
Library of Congress Control Number applied for

Colour reproduction by Evergreen Colour Management Ltd
Printed and bound in China by C&C Offset Printing Co., Ltd

MIX
Paper | Supporting responsible forestry
FSC® C008047